STALEY

Drafted: 1st Round, 8/6/03

Height: Not your average sized bear

Weight: Heavier than you!

Birthplace: Near a lake, in a forest

Jersey #: Double Zero!

Favorite Food: Fish, honey, Chicago-style deep-dish pizza,
Polish Sausage, and Cheese- Heads

Favorite Baseball Team: Cubs...Hello, he's a bear!

About Staley:

Staley is responsible for entertaining Bears fans young and
old. Staley loves to "bust-a-move" and shake what his mama
gave him. He is highly skilled with a fishing pole, enjoys
playing the drums, and exercising regularly. Staley is
best friends with Pooh, Smokey, and Yogi. His former
girlfriend is Britney Sbears.

To book Staley for an appearance call 847-615-9600 or
visit www.chicagobears.com/staley

Let's Go, Bears!

Featuring
Staley

Aimee Aryal

Illustrated by Miguel De Angel

with Brad Vinson

MASCOT
BOOKS®
www.mascotbooks.com

It was a beautiful fall day in Chicago. Bears fans from all over the area were making their way to Soldier Field to watch their beloved Chicago Bears play football.

All over town, everyone dressed in Bears colors. As fans made their way to the stadium, they cheered, "Let's go, Bears!"

Hours before the start of the game, Bears fans began gathering at the stadium. The smell of good food was in the air as smoke billowed from grills. Staley, the Bears' mascot, joined fans in the parking lot. Everyone loved seeing Staley!

Bears fans were eager to show
their spirit. Some children, and even
a few grown-ups, painted their
faces for the game!

As fans made their way through
the stadium gates, they cheered,
"Let's go, Bears!"

The team gathered in the locker room before the game. Players strapped on their pads and dressed in their classic Chicago Bears uniforms. The players felt proud to be a part of the team's championship tradition.

The coach delivered final instructions and encouraged the team to play their best. The coach cheered, "Let's go, Bears!"

It was now time for the Bears to take the field.
The announcer called, "Ladies and gentlemen,
please welcome your Chicago Bears!"
Led by Staley, the team sprinted onto the field.
The Bears were greeted by their loyal fans.
It sure was loud in the stadium!

The Bears huddled around their team captains
and cheered, "Let's go, Bears!"

The team captains met at midfield for the coin toss. The referee flipped a coin high in the air and the visiting team called, "Heads!" The coin landed with the heads side up – the Bears would begin the game by kicking off.

The referee reminded the players that it was important to play hard, but also with good sportsmanship.

The Bears kicker booted the ball down the field to start the action. With the game underway, the kicker cheered, "Let's go, Bears!"

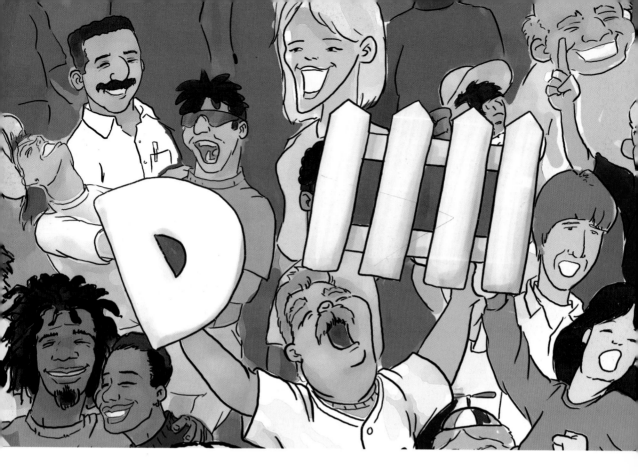

After the opening kickoff, it was time for the
Bears defense to take the field. Staley and
the crowd helped the Bears establish a true
home-field advantage.

A fan held a "D" in one hand and a picket fence
in the other. The crowd chanted, "DE-FENSE!"
With the crowd's encouragement, the Bears
sacked the quarterback. Fans cheered,
"Let's go, Bears!"

The team appreciated the great support they
received from their fans. Bears victories always
included four phases: offense, defense, special
teams, and finally the "Fourth Phase," the fans.

After the defense did a good job, the Bears offense went to work. With great teamwork, they marched down the field. On fourth down, the team was only one yard away from the end zone.

"Let's go for it!" instructed the coach, and the quarterback called a play in the huddle.

"Down! Set! Hike!" yelled the quarterback before handing the ball to the team's running back. With a burst of energy, the running back crossed the goal line. TOUCHDOWN!

To celebrate, fans chanted, "Let's go, Bears!"

At the end of the first half, the Bears
headed back to the locker room. The
coach stopped to answer a few questions
from a television reporter. In the
locker room, the team rested and
prepared for the second half.

Meanwhile, Bears fans stretched their
legs and picked up a few snacks at the
concession stands. Staley mingled with
fans and his antics made everyone laugh!

In the concourse, Bears fans cheered,
"Let's go, Bears!"

Once the second half started, the temperature began
to drop and a chill was in the air. The players played
through the cold conditions. Young Bears fans drank
hot chocolate to help them stay warm. One little
fan was surprised to see herself on the video screen.
With the whole stadium watching, she cheered,
"Let's go, Bears!"

With only a few ticks of the clock remaining, the score was tied. The Bears lined up for a game-winning field goal. The kicker launched the football toward the goal posts. The stadium was nearly silent as all eyes followed the flight of the ball.

The ball sailed between the goal posts. The kick was good! The Bears won the football game! Staley danced in the end zone as the entire stadium chanted, "Let's go, Bears!"

To celebrate the thrilling victory, Bears players gave the head coach an unexpected shower! Of course, Staley was right in the middle of the fun.

The teams then shook hands and congratulated each other on a good game. As Bears fans left the stadium, they cheered, "Let's go, Bears!"

For Anna and Maya. ~ Aimee Aryal

For Sue, Mico, Ana Milagros, and Angel Miguel. ~ Miguel De Angel

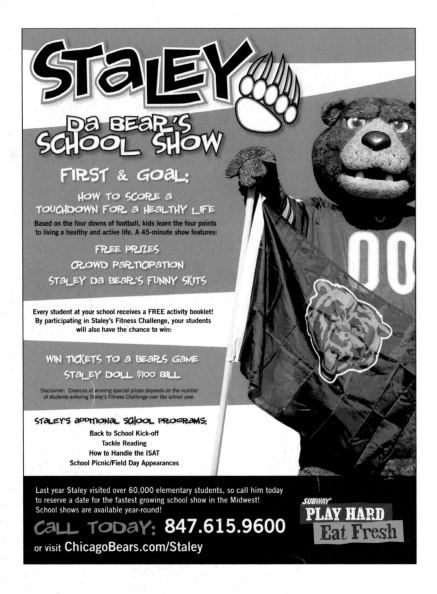

For more information, please contact Mascot Books,
P.O. Box 220157, Chantilly, VA 20153-0157

ISBN: 1-932888-22-5

Title List

Major League Baseball

Boston Red Sox	Hello, *Wally*!	Jerry Remy
Boston Red Sox	*Wally The Green Monster And His Journey Through Red Sox Nation!*	Jerry Remy
Boston Red Sox	Coast to Coast with *Wally The Green Monster*	Jerry Remy
Boston Red Sox	A Season with *Wally The Green Monster*	Jerry Remy
Colorado Rockies	Hello, *Dinger*!	Aimee Aryal
Detroit Tigers	Hello, *Paws*!	Aimee Aryal
New York Yankees	Let's Go, *Yankees*!	Yogi Berra
New York Yankees	*Yankees Town*	Aimee Aryal
New York Mets	Hello, *Mr. Met*!	Rusty Staub
New York Mets	*Mr. Met* and his Journey Through the Big Apple	Aimee Aryal
St. Louis Cardinals	Hello, *Fredbird*!	Ozzie Smith
Philadelphia Phillies	Hello, *Phillie Phanatic*!	Aimee Aryal
Chicago Cubs	Let's Go, *Cubs*!	Aimee Aryal
Chicago White Sox	Let's Go, *White Sox*!	Aimee Aryal
Cleveland Indians	Hello, *Slider*!	Bob Feller
Seattle Mariners	Hello, *Mariner Moose*!	Aimee Aryal
Washington Nationals	Hello, *Screech*!	Aimee Aryal
Milwaukee Brewers	Hello, *Bernie Brewer*!	Aimee Aryal

College

Alabama	Hello, Big Al!	Aimee Aryal
Alabama	Roll Tide!	Ken Stabler
Alabama	Big Al's Journey Through the Yellowhammer State	Aimee Aryal
Arizona	Hello, Wilbur!	Lute Olson
Arkansas	Hello, Big Red!	Aimee Aryal
Arkansas	Big Red's Journey Through the Razorback State	Aimee Aryal
Auburn	Hello, Aubie!	Aimee Aryal
Auburn	War Eagle!	Pat Dye
Auburn	Aubie's Journey Through the Yellowhammer State	Aimee Aryal
Boston College	Hello, Baldwin!	Aimee Aryal
Brigham Young	Hello, Cosmo!	LaVell Edwards
Cal - Berkeley	Hello, Oski!	Aimee Aryal
Clemson	Hello, Tiger!	Aimee Aryal
Clemson	Tiger's Journey Through the Palmetto State	Aimee Aryal
Colorado	Hello, Ralphie!	Aimee Aryal
Connecticut	Hello, Jonathan!	Aimee Aryal
Duke	Hello, Blue Devil!	Aimee Aryal
Florida	Hello, Albert!	Aimee Aryal
Florida State	Let's Go, 'Noles!	Aimee Aryal
Georgia	Hello, Hairy Dawg!	Aimee Aryal
Georgia	How 'Bout Them Dawgs!	Aimee Aryal
Georgia	Hairy Dawg's Journey Through the Peach State	Vince Dooley
Georgia Tech	Hello, Buzz!	Vince Dooley
Gonzaga	Spike, The Gonzaga Bulldog	Aimee Aryal / Mike Pringle
Illinois	Let's Go, Illini!	
Indiana	Let's Go, Hoosiers!	Aimee Aryal
Iowa	Hello, Herky!	Aimee Aryal
Iowa State	Hello, Cy!	Aimee Aryal
James Madison	Hello, Duke Dog!	Amy DeLashmutt
Kansas	Hello, Big Jay!	Aimee Aryal
Kansas State	Hello, Willie!	Aimee Aryal
Kentucky	Hello, Wildcat!	Dan Walter
LSU	Hello, Mike!	Aimee Aryal
LSU	Mike's Journey Through the Bayou State	Aimee Aryal
Maryland	Hello, Testudo!	
Michigan	Let's Go, Blue!	Aimee Aryal
Michigan State	Hello, Sparty!	Aimee Aryal
Minnesota	Hello, Goldy!	Aimee Aryal
Mississippi	Hello, Colonel Rebel!	Aimee Aryal
Mississippi State	Hello, Bully!	Aimee Aryal

Pro Football

Carolina Panthers	Let's Go, Panthers!	Aimee Aryal
Chicago Bears	Let's Go, Bears!	Aimee Aryal
Dallas Cowboys	How 'Bout Them Cowboys!	Aimee Aryal
Green Bay Packers	Go, Pack, Go!	Aimee Aryal
Kansas City Chiefs	Let's Go, Chiefs!	Aimee Aryal
Minnesota Vikings	Let's Go, Vikings!	Aimee Aryal
New York Giants	Let's Go, Giants!	Aimee Aryal
New York Jets	J-E-T-S! Jets, Jets, Jets!	Aimee Aryal
New England Patriots	Let's Go, Patriots!	Aimee Aryal
Pittsburgh Steelers	Here We Go Steelers!	Aimee Aryal
Seattle Seahawks	Let's Go, Seahawks!	Aimee Aryal
Washington Redskins	Hail To The Redskins!	Aimee Aryal

Basketball

Dallas Mavericks	Let's Go, Mavs!	Mark Cuban
Boston Celtics	Let's Go, Celtics!	Aimee Aryal

Other

Kentucky Derby	White Diamond Runs For The Roses	Aimee Aryal
Marine Corps Marathon	Run, Miles, Run!	Aimee Aryal
Missouri	Hello, Truman!	Aimee Aryal
Nebraska	Hello, Herbie Husker!	Todd Donoho
North Carolina	Hello, Rameses!	Aimee Aryal
North Carolina	Rameses' Journey Through the Tar Heel State	Aimee Aryal
North Carolina St.	Hello, Mr. Wuf!	Aimee Aryal
North Carolina St.	Mr. Wuf's Journey Through North Carolina	Aimee Aryal
Notre Dame	Let's Go, Irish!	
Ohio State	Hello, Brutus!	Aimee Aryal
Ohio State	Brutus' Journey	Aimee Aryal
Oklahoma	Let's Go, Sooners!	Aimee Aryal
Oklahoma State	Hello, Pistol Pete!	Aimee Aryal
Oregon	Go Ducks!	Aimee Aryal
Oregon State	Hello, Benny the Beaver!	Aimee Aryal
Penn State	Hello, Nittany Lion!	Aimee Aryal
Penn State	We Are Penn State!	Aimee Aryal
Purdue	Hello, Purdue Pete!	Joe Paterno
Rutgers	Hello, Scarlet Knight!	Aimee Aryal
South Carolina	Hello, Cocky!	Aimee Aryal
South Carolina	Cocky's Journey Through the Palmetto State	Aimee Aryal
So. California	Hello, Tommy Trojan!	
Syracuse	Hello, Otto!	Aimee Aryal
Tennessee	Hello, Smokey!	Aimee Aryal
Tennessee	Smokey's Journey Through the Volunteer State	Aimee Aryal
Texas	Hello, Hook 'Em!	Aimee Aryal
Texas	Hook 'Em's Journey Through the Lone Star State	Aimee Aryal
Texas A & M	Howdy, Reveille!	Aimee Aryal
Texas A & M	Reveille's Journey Through the Lone Star State	Aimee Aryal
Texas Tech	Hello, Masked Rider!	
UCLA	Hello, Joe Bruin!	Aimee Aryal
Virginia	Hello, CavMan!	Aimee Aryal
Virginia Tech	Hello, Hokie Bird!	Aimee Aryal
Virginia Tech	Yea, It's Hokie Game Day!	Frank Beamer
Virginia Tech	Hokie Bird's Journey Through Virginia	Aimee Aryal
Wake Forest	Hello, Demon Deacon!	Aimee Aryal
Washington	Hello, Harry the Husky!	Aimee Aryal
Washington State	Hello, Butch!	Aimee Aryal
West Virginia	Hello, Mountaineer!	Aimee Aryal
Wisconsin	Hello, Bucky!	Aimee Aryal
Wisconsin	Bucky's Journey Through the Badger State	Aimee Aryal

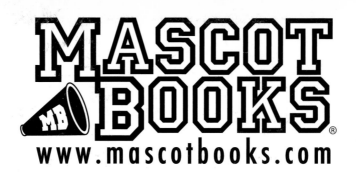
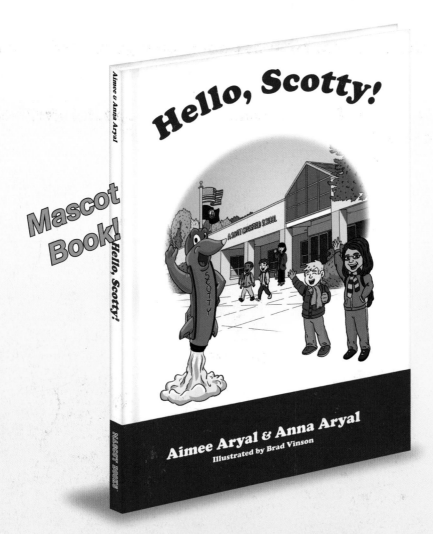